The Littlest Valentine

Written by
Brandi Dougherty

Illustrated by
Michelle Lisa Todd

Cartwheel Books
An Imprint of Scholastic Inc.

For Charlie — my new little valentine. — B.D.

For my special niece, Emily. Love from Auntie Shelley. — M.L.T.

Text copyright © 2017 by Brandi Dougherty
Illustrations copyright © 2017 by Michelle Lisa Todd

Scholastic Inc., 557 Broadway, New York, NY 10012
Scholastic UK Ltd., Euston House, 24 Eversholt Street, London NW1 1DB, United Kingdom

ISBN 978-1-338-15739-0

10 9 8 7 6 5 4 3   18 19 20 21

Printed in the U.S.A.   40
First printing, December 2017

Designed by Jess Tice-Gilbert

Emma Valentine was a girl.
She lived with her family in a big city.
There were many people in Emma's family,

but she was the littlest one.

It was almost Valentine's Day and Emma was excited.
After all, her family's *name* was Valentine.
Valentine's Day was their favorite holiday!

The Valentines owned a gift shop where people
bought their Valentine's Day gifts and treats.
And this year Emma would join the family business.
She couldn't wait to help!

Emma joined her brother, Elliot, with the heart-shaped balloons. But there wasn't enough air in her little lungs to fill a balloon.

"Emma, are you okay?" Elliot asked. "You don't look so good."
"I'm fine," Emma wheezed.
"I think you're too little to help with the balloons," Elliot replied.
"Try making cards instead."

Emma's parents were in their workshop making Valentine's Day cards.
"I'd like to make a card," Emma whispered.
She picked up a small scrap of pink paper and got to work.

"How's this?" she asked, holding up her creation.
"That's very cute, sweetheart," Emma's mom said.
"But I'm afraid it's kind of small."

"Want to try again?" her dad asked. "Or you could help Nana and Poppy."

Emma decided to go see her grandparents in the kitchen.
"Hello, Emma!" Poppy boomed when she arrived.
"Here to make some chocolates?"
"Yes, I am!" Emma smiled. She had a good feeling about chocolate making.

Nana showed Emma how to
squeeze chocolate onto a tray.

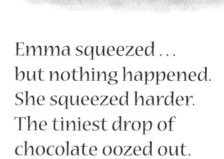

Emma squeezed ...
but nothing happened.
She squeezed harder.
The tiniest drop of
chocolate oozed out.

Poppy handed Emma a truffle.
"You should try balloons!" he offered.
"I already did." Emma sighed.

Emma stomped outside.
She was sad and a bit grumpy.
Emma knew there had to be one Valentine job she could do,
even if she was little.

Then Emma heard a noise.
There, on the other side of the fence, was a puppy.
He looked sad and a bit grumpy.

And he was little, just like Emma!

Emma approached the fence, but the puppy backed away.
He was muddy and wet. And he didn't have a collar.
"It's okay," Emma said gently.

Emma ran inside and came back
with a small bowl of food.
The puppy came right over.
He was hungry!

She opened the gate.
The puppy walked
to the bowl to eat.
Emma smiled.

Nana and Poppy came out to see what was keeping Emma so busy.
"Can we keep him?" Emma asked her grandparents.
"Maybe," said Nana. "Let's call the animal shelter first
and make sure no one is looking for him."

Emma led the puppy into the house.
She ran a warm bath with extra bubbles while
Nana called the animal shelter.

Emma scrubbed and scrubbed.
Soon he was shiny and clean.

Nana came in. "Looks like this puppy needs a home."
Emma smiled. "Your name is Eek," she told the puppy.
"And you live here now."
Eek wagged his tail happily.

Emma found a thick red ribbon with hearts on it to tie around Eek's neck.
The ribbon reminded her that it was almost Valentine's Day.
Then she had an idea. "Come on, Eek, we've got work to do!"

Emma went into the kitchen and asked Nana and Poppy for help.
They set to work making heart-shaped dog treats.
Eek was the taste-tester.

Before long, the whole Valentine family was gathered in the kitchen filling bags of treats for the gift shop.

Emma's dad set up a stand in the corner of the shop
for Emma and Eek to sell their treats.
The treats were a huge hit with the customers —
especially the furry ones!

"What a wonderful idea," Emma's mom said.
"What made you think of it?"
"Everybody needs a little love on Valentine's Day," Emma replied.

Emma had found her special Valentine job after all.
But more than that, she had also found a special friend.